ADVENTURES

The Round Table

Tales of King Arthur

First published in 2006 by
Franklin Watts
338 Euston Road
London
NW1 3BH

Franklin Watts Australia
Hachette Children's Books
Level 17/207 Kent Street
Sydney
NSW 2000

A CIP catalogue record for this book is available
from the British Library.

ISBN (10) 0 7496 6684 6 (hbk)
ISBN (13) 978-0-7496-6684-2 (hbk)
ISBN (10) 0 7496 6697 8 (pbk)
ISBN (13) 978-0-7496-6697-2 (pbk)

Series Editor: Jackie Hamley
Series Advisor: Dr Barrie Wade
Series Designer: Peter Scoulding

Printed in China

Franklin Watts is a division of
Hachette Childen's Books.

To Jackie, with love
and thanks – K.W.

The Round Table

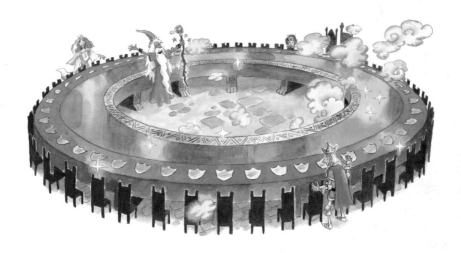

by Karen Wallace and Neil Chapman

FRANKLIN WATTS
LONDON • SYDNEY

For the first time in many years,
there was peace in Britain.

King Arthur and his knights had
finally defeated all the outlaws
and witches who had been
causing trouble in the land.

"Now I would like to find a wife
and have children," said Arthur.

One day, on his way back to
Camelot, he met a beautiful woman.

Her name was Guinevere and they fell in love at first sight.

Guinevere's father agreed to the
marriage and they made a plan
to marry as soon as possible.

When Arthur arrived back at his castle, he held a feast for his knights.

A long table was placed in the
Great Hall and delicious food
and drink was set out.

But as soon as the knights began to take their places, an argument broke out among them.

Everyone wanted to sit at the top of the table near King Arthur.

No one wanted to sit at the bottom.

"Silence!" cried Merlin the magician. "When Guinevere becomes Queen I shall make a special table, shaped like a circle!"

Merlin held up his hand. "It will
be called the Round Table of
Camelot. There will be no more
arguments over who sits where!"

Soon King Arthur and the Lady Guinevere were married. All the knights in the land came to wish them well.

18

After the wedding, Merlin summoned the new King and Queen to the Great Hall.

Then he waved his wand and spun round in a circle. The room was filled with a blazing light.

Suddenly a huge gleaming table
appeared. "Look!" cried Merlin.
"The Round Table I promised you!"

Arthur was amazed. All the names
of his knights were written around
the edge!

"There are places for you and
Queen Guinevere and for all your
knights," said Merlin. "When a
new knight comes to serve you,
his name will appear on the
table by magic."

King
Arthur

24

25

That night everyone took their places for the wedding feast, and this time there was no argument about who sat where.

But Merlin did not sit down.

"It is time for me to leave you,"

he told Arthur.

"Watch over your kingdom and remember this table marks the beginning of many adventures." Then Merlin disappeared!

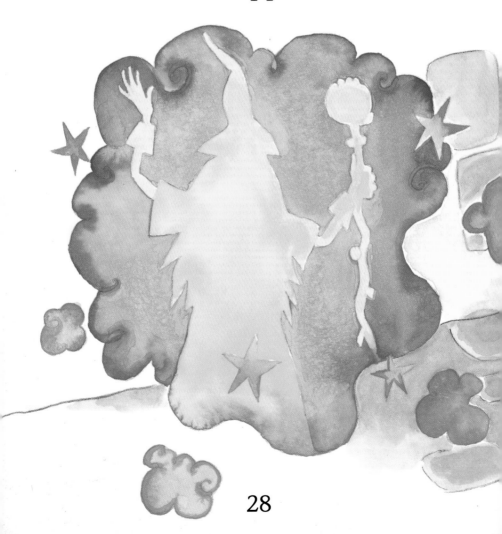

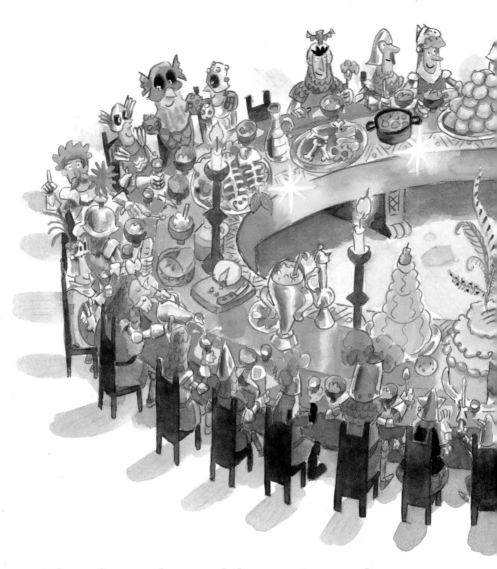

The feast lasted long into the
night, but Arthur already
missed his friend.

As he thought of Merlin, the
great Round Table gleamed
more brightly than ever.

Hopscotch has been specially designed to fit the requirements of the National Literacy Strategy. It offers real books by top authors and illustrators for children developing their reading skills. There are 37 Hopscotch stories to choose from:

Marvin, the Blue Pig
ISBN 0 7496 4619 5

Plip and Plop
ISBN 0 7496 4620 9

The Queen's Dragon
ISBN 0 7496 4618 7

Flora McQuack
ISBN 0 7496 4621 7

Willie the Whale
ISBN 0 7496 4623 3

Naughty Nancy
ISBN 0 7496 4622 5

Run!
ISBN 0 7496 4705 1

The Playground Snake
ISBN 0 7496 4706 X

"Sausages!"
ISBN 0 7496 4707 8

The Truth about Hansel and Gretel
ISBN 0 7496 4708 6

Pippin's Big Jump
ISBN 0 7496 4710 8

Whose Birthday Is It?
ISBN 0 7496 4709 4

The Princess and the Frog
ISBN 0 7496 5129 6

Flynn Flies High
ISBN 0 7496 5130 X

Clever Cat
ISBN 0 7496 5131 8

Moo!
ISBN 0 7496 5332 9

Izzie's Idea
ISBN 0 7496 5334 5

Roly-poly Rice Ball
ISBN 0 7496 5333 7

I Can't Stand It!
ISBN 0 7496 5765 0

Cockerel's Big Egg
ISBN 0 7496 5767 7

How to Teach a Dragon Manners
ISBN 0 7496 5873 8

The Truth about those Billy Goats
ISBN 0 7496 5766 9

Marlowe's Mum and the Tree House
ISBN 0 7496 5874 6

Bear in Town
ISBN 0 7496 5875 4

The Best Den Ever
ISBN 0 7496 5876 2

ADVENTURE STORIES

Aladdin and the Lamp
ISBN 0 7496 6678 1 *
ISBN 0 7496 6692 7

Blackbeard the Pirate
ISBN 0 7496 6676 5 *
ISBN 0 7496 6690 0

George and the Dragon
ISBN 0 7496 6677 3 *
ISBN 0 7496 6691 9

Jack the Giant-Killer
ISBN 0 7496 6680 3 *
ISBN 0 7496 6693 5

TALES OF KING ARTHUR

1. The Sword in the Stone
ISBN 0 7496 6681 1 *
ISBN 0 7496 6694 3

2. Arthur the King
ISBN 0 7496 6683 8 *
ISBN 0 7496 6695 1

3. The Round Table
ISBN 0 7496 6684 6 *
ISBN 0 7496 6697 8

4. Sir Lancelot and the Ice Castle
ISBN 0 7496 6685 4 *
ISBN 0 7496 6698 6

TALES OF ROBIN HOOD

Robin and the Knight
ISBN 0 7496 6686 2 *
ISBN 0 7496 6699 4

Robin and the Monk
ISBN 0 7496 6687 0 *
ISBN 0 7496 6700 1

Robin and the Friar
ISBN 0 7496 6688 9 *
ISBN 0 7496 6702 8

Robin and the Silver Arrow
ISBN 0 7496 6689 7 *
ISBN 0 7496 6703 6

* hardback